This book belongs to:

_____

HOORAY FOR HAT!

Words and pictures by

Brian Won

Andersen Press

For Leny and Charlie

This paperback first published in Great Britain in 2014 by Andersen Press Ltd., 20 Vauxhall Bridge Road, London SW1V 2SA.

Published in Australia by Random House Australia Pty., Level 3, 100 Pacific Highway, North Sydney, NSW 2060. Copyright © 2014 Brian Won.

Published by special arrangement with Houghton Mifflin Harcourt Publishing Company, and Rights People, London.

The rights of Brian Won to be identified as the author and illustrator of this work have been asserted

by him in accordance with the Copyright, Designs and Patents Act, 1988.

All rights reserved.

Printed and bound in Malaysia by Tien Wah Press. British Library Cataloguing in Publication Data available.

ISBN 978 1 78344 176 1

10 9 8 7 6 5 4 3 2 1

When Elephant woke up, he was very grumpy.

The doorbell rang.

Elephant stomped down the stairs.

"GO AWAY!

I'M GRUMPY!"

There was a present on the doorstep!

Elephant unwrapped the box.

It was hard to stay grumpy now.

"HOORAY FOR HAT!"

Elephant cheered.

"I will show Zebra!"

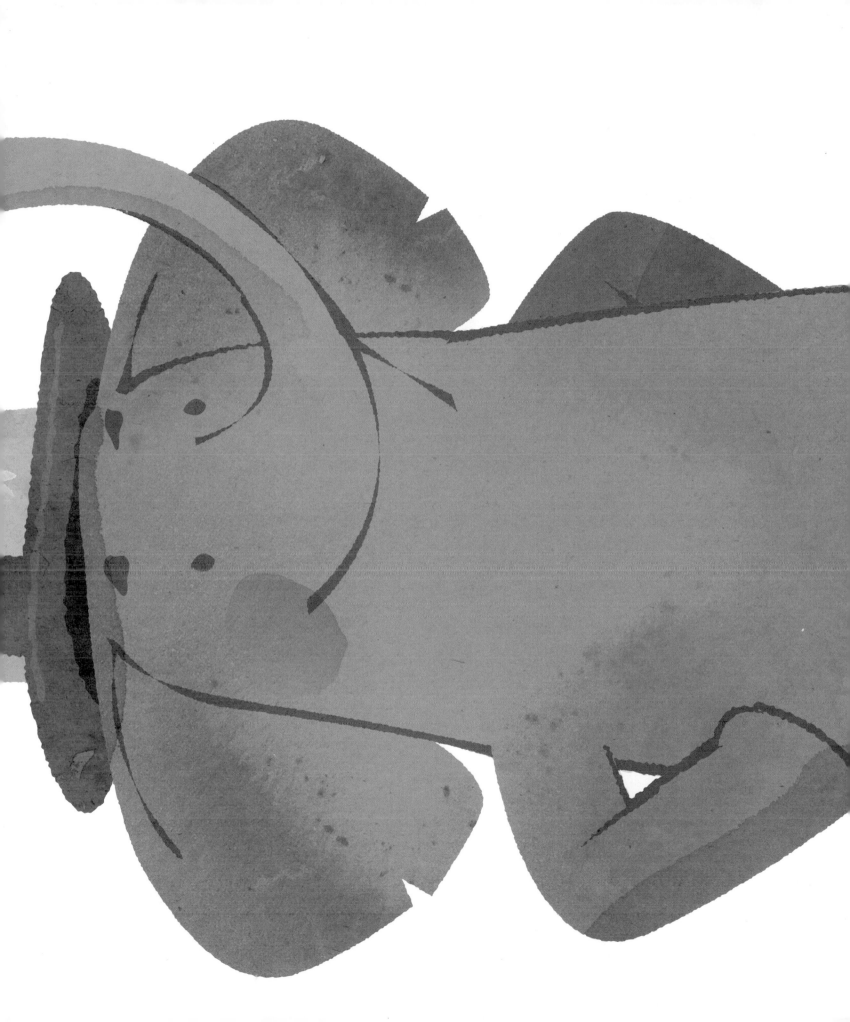

But Zebra did not want to look at any hats.

"GO AWAY!

I'M GRUMPY!"

So Elephant gave Zebra a hat.

Zebra smiled. They both cheered,

"HOORAY FOR HAT!

Let's show Turtle!"

But Turtle would not come out of his shell.

"GO AWAY!
I'M GRUMPY!"

Elephant gave Turtle a hat too.

Turtle smiled. They all cheered,

"HOORAY FOR HAT!

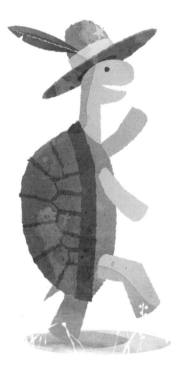

Let's show Owl!"

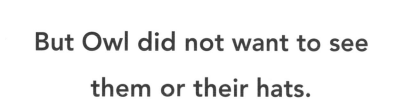

But Owl did not want to see
them or their hats.

"GO AWAY!
I'M GRUMPY!"

Elephant gave Owl a hat too.
Owl smiled. They all cheered,

"HOO-HOO-HOORAY FOR HAT!"

Elephant, Zebra, Turtle, and Owl
marched down the road to show Lion.

"HO

ORAY
FOR HAT!"

But Lion did not want any visitors.

"GO AWAY!

I'M GRUMPY!"

Elephant gave Lion a hat too. But Lion was still sad.
"I love this hat. But I can't cheer while our friend
Giraffe is not feeling well. What can we do?"

So Elephant, Zebra, Turtle, Owl,
and Lion made a surprise for Giraffe.

They all marched to Giraffe's home.

On the way, Lion started to feel better.

And soon . . .

. . . Giraffe felt better too.

You might also enjoy:

9781783441556

9781849397803